Cover design by **Holly Symons**
First Edition

For More, Please Visit

HollySymons.com.au

The Realmsverse Codex

A Canonical Record of the Known Characters from Realms One through Eleven

Compiled under the Watch of the Guardian of the Scroll

Author's Note

from the Temporary (but Determined) Chronicler of the Realms

Hello, Brave reader.

This book was never supposed to exist. Not because it wasn't needed, but because the Realms rarely sit still long enough to be documented. Every time I finished a sentence, someone rewrote history. Or exploded it. Or turned it into a very loud musical involving dragons, glitter, and snacks.

Still, here it is a labour of love, chaos, and far too many arguments with enchanted quills.

These pages are filled with truth, myth, and the occasional talking squirrel footnote. Some characters will become your friends. Some will test your patience. All of them are real... somewhere.

I wrote this for the adventurers who feel out of

place in their own story. For the scribblers who've lost their plots. For the quiet rebels. And especially for anyone who's ever asked, "What if...?"

Thank you for opening the Codex. You're part of it now.

And no, you can't give it back.

With ink-stained fingers and a hopeful grin,
H.S.
Officially Unofficial Guardian of Lore

The Realmsverse Codex – Table of Contents

Author's Note

Table of Contents

Foundational Lore Section

- The Realms

- The Ancient Author

Character Biographies

- Aurelya – The Guardian of the Scroll

- Aurelya – The Rewrite Awakened

- Aurexia – The Rewrite Queen

- Belladonna – The Poisoned Muse

- Captain Belladonna's Vex – The Curse of the Indigo Sea

- Chad – Goblin Life Coach (Certified. Somehow.)

- Clarence – The Lion (Don't Call Him a Cat)

- Dr. Vexandra Bloomfield – Mistress of Alchemical Botany

- The Dragon – Emberwing, Keeper of the Flame verse

- Fake Aurelya – The Crown-Wearing Impostor

- Fraya – The Lorebound Seer of Threads

- Gerald

- Gliffin – The Rogue Line-Editor

- Hero – The One Who Never Showed Up

- Judge Chad – Keeper of Emotional Trials

- Kaelun – The One Who Knows (Elf)

- Kevin – The Suspiciously Normal Intern

- Loki (Loki Laufeyson)

- Loki Squirrel – Sir Claws-a-Lot

- Mirror Gerald

- The Minotaur

- Nyra

- Nyric

- Odin

- Plottie™

- Princess Parenthesis – The Parenthetical Powerhouse

- Princess Rhymelda

- Roarnan – The Quiet Flame

- Sir Broodington III

- Sir Broodington the Third

- Sir Tangent the Derailer

- Sparkles Roarworthy

- The Squirrel Council

- Sir Scribbles – Presiding Judge of the Final Rewrite

- The Sea Witch

- Thor – God of Thunderous Overcompensations

- Thor's Chickens – The Feathered Flock of Thunder

- Trystan – The Reluctant Prince of Plotlines

- The Villain Ex

- Varyn

- Veylion – The Mirror's Shadow

- Veyrath – The Flamebound Guardian

Realm Dwellers & Groups

- The Forge Dwarfs – Makers of Myth and Metal

- The Dwarf

- The Elves – Whisperers of Wonder and Waffles

- Gary

- Species: Chaos Squirrel (Possibly)

- Odin's Goat – Buttermunch the Thunderous

- The Samurai Otters – Guardians of the Ripple Code

- The Shakespearean Penguins – Troupe of the Frostbitten Bard

- Sir Crumbs

- Spikeston the Impenetrable

- The Giants – Gentle Hulks of the High Hills

- The Masked Ones

- The Talking Cactus

- The Witnesses

- The Time-Tossed Jury

- Closure the Cloaked Raccoon (Mascot)

- Spiny the Bartender – Keeper of Drinks and Secrets

- Whiffles

Realm Locations

- The Tree of Life

- The Book Tree

- The Library

- The School for Emotionally Unavailable Side Characters

- "The Misrule Inn" – Loki's Tavern

- A Ship Named Emotional Baggage – Vessel of Chaotic Healing

Magical Items & Events

- The Scroll

- The Mirror

- The Author's Mirror

- The Thread

- The Prophecy Eggs

- The Tapas Table

- A Mood Ring

- The Glitter Bomb

- The Enchanted Crayons

- Chad's Therapy Crystals™

Legendary Weapons & Artefacts

- The Pen

- The Pen of Obsidian

- The Sentient Sword

- Mjölnir

- The Crown

Bonus Lore or Secret Lore Section

- Deleted Characters Unwritten, Unhinged, and Unapologetically Cut

- Deleted Selves

- The Crayons Rebel

- This one is... a Reader

- The Author – Just a Woman

- The Forgotten Gerald

- The Narrator

Foundational
Lore

Foundational Lore

The Realms

*Ten worlds. One story. Always rewriting. *

The Realms are older than time,
and yet somehow always younger than yesterday.

Born from the First Story ever told,
Each Realm reflects a part of the soul:
- A Realm of Fire and Forgetting.
- A Realm of Ice and Memory.
- A Realm where logic whispers in rhyme.
- And another where dragons debate bureaucracy.

Some Realms are ruled by kings.
Others by chaos.
One by a council of squirrels.

But all are bound by one thread:
The Rewrite.

When a story grows too tangled,
when a prophecy unravels,
When a hero forgets who they were meant to be
The Realms shift.

Maps redraw.
Stars blink out.
And somewhere, someone finds a quill they didn't know they
dropped.

The Realms aren't just a place.
They're a possibility.
And the only way through them…

is to rewrite.

The Ancient Author

Name:

Unknown (The Realms call them "The Ancient Author")

Realm:

Allegedly born outside all Ten,' from before the First Realm'

Species/Role:

Reality Scribe / Creator / Hermit of Ink

Known For:

Writing the original Scroll of Realms. Disappearing mid-story. Possibly hiding inside the Library That Eats Endings.

Allegiances & Conflicts:

Created the original laws of the Realms... then broke them. Hunted by rewrite forces, protected by plot holes.

Notable Quote:

"I never meant to make it real. I just wanted to see if the words would listen."

Realmsverse Note:

Some claim the Ancient Author can be summoned by writing the perfect metaphor at midnight. Others say they are already watching... from the margins.

Aurelya – The Guardian of the Scroll

Name:

Aurelya – The Guardian of the scroll

Realm:

Realm One

Species/Role:

Elven Guardian

Known For:

Serenity, leadership, and her bond with the Scroll of Realms. Aurelya is known for her light-gold hair, elegant poise, and unwavering duty to keep the balance between Realms.

Allegiances & Conflicts:

Trusted by the Witnesses, often in conflict with Loki's improvisations, and forever linked to Gerald the Bard.

Notable Quote:

"The Realms must be preserved… even if it breaks my heart to do so."

Aurelya – The Rewrite Awakened

Name:

Aurelya – The Rewrite Awakened

Realm:

All Realms (Post-Rewrite)

Species/Role:

Living Rewrite / Guardian Ascended

Known For:

Fiery red hair that appeared when she rewrote her fate. Known now for raw magical force, soul-deep intuition, and choosing her own path beyond prophecy.

Allegiances & Conflicts:

Wrestles with the legacy of Aurexia. Bound to the Scroll and the fate of Loki. Battles internal guilt for choosing power over peace.

Notable Quote:

"I didn't fall from the Tree of Life… I climbed down. And I rewrote what I found waiting for me."

Aurexia – The Rewrite Queen

Name:

Aurexia – The Rewrite Queen

Realm:

Unknown (Fragmented from Aurelya across the Realms)

Species/Role:

Shard-Born Rewrite / Queen of the Unwritten

Known For:

Rewriting reality to suit her vision of 'perfection'.
Master manipulator and cosmic strategist, her magic
manifests as black ink that 'bleeds' into the world she
reshapes.

Allegiances & Conflicts:

Claims loyalty to the Realms but reshapes them at will.
Waged ink storm wars against the Witnesses. Obsessed
with reclaiming Aurelya's crown or proving she
deserved it all along.

Notable Quote:

"I wasn't born. I was edited. And I intend to rewrite
everything, including you."

Realmsverse Note:

It is believed Aurexia formed during the split at the
Tree, a reaction to Aurelya's self-doubt, the version that
didn't climb down. She is not evil… just unfinished.

Belladonna – The Poisoned Muse

Name:

Belladonna

Title:

The Poisoned Muse

Realm:

The Garden of Tangles (hidden within Realm Four or Five)

Species/Role:

Fae Alchemist / Whisper Witch / Former Love Interest of…
someone… probably everyone

Known For:

Poison-laced poetry. Bottling emotions into perfume vials.
Giving people advice that sounds helpful until Act III.

Allegiances & Conflicts:

Sometimes allies with Aurexia, sometimes feeds her bad
tea. Loki might be in love with her. Or maybe she's in love
with herself.

Notable Quote:

"It's not poison if you enjoy the way it burns."

Realmsverse Note:

Belladonna's garden is said to rearrange itself depending
on who enters. No one can find the same path twice. Except
the chicken. But he's not talking.

Captain Belladonna's Vex –
The Curse of the Indigo Sea

Name:

Captain Belladonna's Vex

Title:

The Curse of the Indigo Sea

Realm:

The Shattered Shoals (between Realm 6 & Realm 7, though he swears it moves)

Species/Role:

Pirate Lord / Cursed Navigator / Belladonna's Ex-Whatever

Known For:

Steering a ship that shouldn't float. Laughing during lightning storms. Having once stolen a memory and returned it better.

Allegiances & Conflicts:

Loyal to his crew. Deadly to most others. Was probably cursed by Belladonna. Still writes her letters.

Notable Quote:

"I never lied to her. I just told the truth with better lighting."

Realmsverse Note:

It's unclear if "Vex" is his name, his ship, or his fate. He never answers directly. He just smiles.

Chad – Goblin Life Coach
(Certified. Somehow.)

Name:

Chad

Title:

Goblin Life Coach (Certified. Somehow.)

Realm:

Realm Nine, but he's been "trying out some new frequencies lately."

Species/Role:

Goblin / Therapist / Motivational Scream Artist

Known For:

Giving unsolicited advice that accidentally saves kingdoms. Running the Realms' most chaotic group therapy sessions. Owning three lava lamps and one ethically sourced emotional support rock.

Allegiances & Conflicts:

Was hired by Gerald, tolerated by Thor, and deeply respected by chickens. Has been banned from at least two realms for trying to "align the ley lines with positive affirmation."

Notable Quote:

"You're not a plot hole. You're a rewrite opportunity with glitter potential."

Realmsverse Note:

Chad's qualifications have never been verified, but he *does* have a clipboard and once made Odin cry (in a good way).

Clarence – The Lion (Don't Call Him a Cat)

Name:

Clarence

Title:

The Lion (Don't Call Him a Cat)

Realm:

Originally, Realm Two now travels beside Aurelya

Species/Role:

Lion Companion / Royal Advisor / Emotional Support Roar

Known For:

Sitting in perfect silence during dramatic monologues. Growling at anyone who tries to cut Aurelya off mid-sentence. Once fought a metaphor and won.

Allegiances & Conflicts:

Fiercely loyal to Aurelya. Has a mild rivalry with Gerald (over who gets the armchair). Intimidated the squirrel once. It's still a sore subject.

Notable Quote:

*(He doesn't speak. But if he did, it would probably be something like…) *
"I said nothing. And you understood everything."

Realmsverse Note:

Clarence may or may not be more than a lion. Some speculate he is a fragment of the Tree's will. Others just think he's had enough of everyone's nonsense.

Dr. Vexandra Bloomfield – Mistress of Alchemical Botany

Name:

Dr. Vexandra Bloomfield

Title:

Mistress of Alchemical Botany / Lecturer in Occult Floral Manipulation

Realm:

Realm Six – University of Vine & Veil (Tenure unclear, as the building keeps relocating)

Species/Role:

Fae-kin / Academic, Floromancer, and Unlicensed Therapist

Known For:

• Brewing mood-altering teas that may or may not whisper your secrets aloud.
• Planting explosive snapdragons in the Chancellor's rose garden.
• Once convinced a cactus it was royalty.

Allegiances & Conflicts:

• Considered a frenemy of Belladonna.
• Banned from two Realms for "unauthorised vine invasions."
• Trusted by those who have no other choice.

Notable Quote:

"Therapy is just horticulture with better metaphors."

Realmsverse Note:

Dr. Bloomfield's experiments have often skirted the edge of narrative collapse. Despite this, her lectures are standing room only (sometimes because her plants have claimed the chairs). She remains a controversial figure, revered, feared, and strangely floral.

The Dragon – Emberwing, Keeper of the Flame verse

Name:

Emberwing (The Dragon)

Title:

Keeper of the Flame verse / Guardian of Lore fire

Realm:

Primarily Realm Nine – Though often glimpsed in the skies between stories – Once a mentor to Veyrath, Aurelyas, bonded dragon.

Species/Role:

Dragon / Living Archive of Ancient Flame Lore

Known For:

• Torch-bearing flight over lost chapters.
• Roars that ignite truth and burn away illusions.
• Protecting Aurelya and Clarence with a bond deeper than prophecy.
• Occasionally hoards rare ink bottles and overdramatic scrolls.

Allegiances & Conflicts:

• Fiercely loyal to Aurelya.
• Unspoken rivalry with The Lion over who is more majestic.
• Once roasted a plot hole just for whispering too loud.

Notable Quote:

"I do not breathe fire. I breathe clarity."

Realmsverse Note:

Emberwing's presence signals a pivotal turning point in the realms. The dragon shares an unbreakable bond with Aurelya and Clarence, sometimes even flying with both on its back. Though rarely speaks, its actions write volumes across the skies.

Fake Aurelya – The Crown-Wearing Impostor

Name:

Fake Aurelya (aka 'The Shiny One')

Title:

The Crown-Wearing Impostor / The Almost-Aurelya

Realm:

Realm Eleven – The Realm That Wasn't (Or Shouldn't Be)

Species/Role:

Construct of Narrative Deception / Sentient Plot Misdirection

Known For:

• Stealing Aurelya's look (but missing the emotional depth).
• Hosting parties while the Realms fell apart.
• Gaslighting half the cast into doubting their memories.
• Being suspiciously shiny.

Alliances & Conflicts:

• Allegedly allied with Aurexia.
• Actively resented by Clarence.
• Loki won't speak of her, and that's saying something.

Notable Quote:

"Why rewrite the realms when you can distract them?"

Realmsverse Note:

Fake Aurelya was introduced during the Realm Fracture to serve
as a placeholder while the true Aurelya healed. The problem? She
got a little too comfortable wearing the crown. Though she's
technically harmless, she's also… inconvenient. And unnervingly
charming.

Fraya – The Lorebound
Seer of Threads

Name:

Fraya

Title:

The Lorebound Seer / Weaver of Futures That Might Be

Realm:

Dwells at the edge of Realm Two and the Threadways

Species/Role:

Prophetic Entity / Keeper of the Loom of Echoed Fates

Known For:

• Speaking in riddles, usually while doing embroidery.
• Brewing tea that somehow reveals your deepest truths.
• Guiding heroes — and villains — toward threads they're not
ready to face.
• Knitting entire timelines into scarves (fashionable and
devastating).

Alliances & Conflicts:

• Sworn neutral yet oddly invested in Aurelya's fate.
• Once refused to help Aurexia, then regretted nothing.
• Rumoured to have tangled fates with Chad in a lost novella.

Notable Quote:

"I don't predict. I prepare."

Realmsverse Note:

Fraya exists beyond judgment. Her gift is clarity — whether you
want it or not. She sees the branching of stories like threads in a
tapestry, and her every word is a stitch that nudges fate forward...
or back.

Gerald

Name:

Gerald

Title:

The Bureaucratic Bard

Role:

Lore-Keeper of the Plot Department

Bio:

Gerald is the overworked, under-caffeinated administrator of Realm Regulations, stuck trying to file magical paperwork while the Realms fall into chaos. A chronic note-taker with a mild fear of glitter, he secretly dreams of writing his own epic. Unfortunately, he's stuck editing everyone else's storylines. Loyal to a fault, easily flustered, and occasionally brilliant, Gerald often stumbles into heroism by sheer accident. He can recite copyright laws in his sleep, always carries twelve types of ink, and once accidentally summoned a thunderstorm by overthinking a metaphor. He did not sign up for this mess, but he's the only one keeping the narrative from collapsing in on itself.

GLIFFIN

Gliffin – The Rogue Line-Editor

Gliffin once served as the Realmsverse's chief line-editor, armed with a mighty red quill that struck terror into the hearts of verbose bards and rambling narrators.

Once a loyal servant of narrative clarity, Gliffin snapped during a footnote rebellion. Now rogue, he roams the margins, striking out commas, correcting spelling errors mid-battle, and leaving passive-aggressive sticky notes on destiny scrolls.

He wears a cloak made of rejected manuscripts and carries a grammar grimoire that hums with pedantic energy. Some say he speaks only in clauses and never forgets a misplaced modifier.

Enemies: Chad (for his relaxed use of adjectives), Jerald (for refusing to proofread). Friends: Semi-colons.

Weakness: Irregular verbs in the present perfect subjunctive.

Hero – The One Who Never Showed Up

Hero was supposed to be the chosen one.

Prophecies foretold his arrival with a shimmering sword, a tragic backstory, and an impeccable jawline. The Realmsverse trained narrators for years to herald his destiny, entire plot arcs were put on pause… and yet? He ghosted the story.

No letter. No scroll. No dramatic entrance.

Some say he tripped over the tutorial level and rage-quit the Realms. Others believe he's just 'taking time to find himself' in a side plot somewhere near the Realm of Self-Discovery.

His name is still etched in ancient stones, but most characters now use it ironically. 'Nice job, Hero,' they say when someone forgets to untangle a prophecy.

Status: Missing in action.

Likely to return the moment everything's been sorted without him.

Judge Chad – Keeper of Emotional Trials

Once a wandering life coach, now elevated to the emotional court of the Realmsverse, Judge Chad presides over all matters of heartbreak, sibling drama, and unresolved parent issues.

Donning a robe stitched from the fabric of overused metaphors, Judge Chad listens intently, squints meaningfully, and occasionally bangs a gavel made of scented wood. His courtroom is lined with motivational posters, and his sentencing often includes journaling assignments and time-outs in the Room of Reflective Silence.

He was not *technically* licensed when appointed. The scroll was smudged. But nobody had the heart to object.

Famous ruling: Declared 'lack of closure' a valid trauma arc.

Likes: Crystals, compassion, and calling out emotionally unavailable side characters.
Dislikes: Gaslighting, unresolved foreshadowing, and plot holes.

Kaelun

The One Who Knows (Elf)

Kaelun is the quiet thunder in the storm of the Realms. Born under an eclipse and raised among the Timelines, he sees the echoes of every moment past, present, and those not yet chosen.

He rarely speaks unless it matters, and when he does, even Time listens. Burdened with visions of a thousand possible outcomes, Kaelun often bears the sorrow of knowing how things must break... and choosing to stay anyway.

His bond with Aurelya is one of soul threads and slow-burn loyalty. He's not the loudest hero, but he is often the last one standing.

Strengths: Timeline navigation, emotional restraint, looking cool while brooding. Weaknesses: Emotional repression, unresolved feelings, and dragons who eat all the snacks.

Rumours say he once saw the end of everything and smiled anyway.

KEVIN

Kevin – The Suspiciously Normal Intern

Kevin insists he's just an intern.

Shows up every Tuesday, takes meeting notes, refills the Plot Baby's juice box, and somehow avoids getting caught in battle scenes.

Nobody remembers hiring him.

He doesn't seem magical, mythical, or remotely qualified, but he's *always* around. Tidying scrolls. Filing chaos. Listening… too closely.

Some believe Kevin is a disguised deity. Others say he's a glitch in the narrative engine. The Forgotten Bards once wrote a ballad about him, but it vanished overnight.

Known aliases: Kev, Kevin-from-Accounting, and 'Wait, who's Kevin?'

Status: Intern. Probably. (Do not feed after midnight.)

Loki (Loki Laufeyson)

Loki – Trickster of the Realms, Wielder of Wit, and Champion of Chaos

With a smirk that can undo reality and a squirrel that may or may not run a black market in plot twists, Loki thrives in the delightful chaos between order and absurdity. A master shapeshifter and unpredictable ally, he walks the line between friend and frenemy to Aurelya, occasionally stealing the show and the crown, the map, or the cookies.

Wearing sarcasm like armour and wielding shadowy magic with flair, Loki is the reason the plot derailed... and also the reason it kept going. He pretends not to care, but his loyalty (deeply buried under layers of snark) has helped save the Realms more times than anyone will admit. Also: possibly the squirrel's co-conspirator.

Favourite Quote: "I didn't ruin the plot. I improved it."

Loki Squirrel - Sir Claws-a-Lot

Name: Sir Claws-a-Lot

Species: Unclear (Technically a squirrel, spiritually a chaos gremlin)

Affiliation: Loki's sidekick, chaos accomplice, and part-time saboteur of linear storytelling

Appearance:

Sir Claws-a-Lot is a scruffy, wide-eyed squirrel with a tiny helmet, a chestnut-hued tail of epic proportions, and a scar over one eye that nobody knows the origin of (including him). Carries a nut satchel filled with "plot devices." Often perches dramatically on shoulders or curls up in scrolls.

Personality:

– Frequently interrupts serious moments with random acrobatics or unsolicited life advice.

– Speaks only in dramatic squeaks (which Loki insists are intelligible).

Notable Traits:

– Has bitten at least three gods.

– Once ran a black-market subplot exchange behind Chapter Nine.

– Might be cursed? Might be blessed? Definitely hexed someone.

Backstory:
Originally summoned by accident when Loki
tried to create a familiar using poetic metaphors
and fermented apples. Sir Claws-a-Lot clawed his
way into existence and never left. Over time, he's
stolen not just shiny objects, but also scenes,
hearts, and occasionally the narration.

Role in the Realms:
He's everywhere and nowhere. Shows up exactly
when needed and precisely when it's
inconvenient. Some believe he's the true author
behind all chaos in the Realmsverse. Others think
he's just hungry.

Trivia:
– Once stole, Thor's entire lunch and framed
Gerald.
– Has a sworn rivalry with The Plot Baby's duck.
– Collects abandoned punchlines and sharpens
them like weapons.

Status: Loose in the narrative. Do not attempt to
capture.

The Plot Baby's duck

Mirror Gerald

Mirror Gerald is not Gerald's reflection; he's what happens when you ignore self-care, bottle up your feelings, and then try to function like everything is fine. Snarky, suspicious, and with bags under his eyes deeper than most plot holes, Mirror Gerald is the living embodiment of burnout with flair.

Unlike Gerald's usual optimism, Mirror Gerald prefers pessimistic realism: if the worst can happen, it probably will. He speaks in passive-aggressive motivational quotes and once tried to run a 'Self-Sabotage Support Group' but accidentally gaslit himself into not showing up.

Abilities:
• Can reflect your worst traits, whether you asked or not.
• Excellent at deflecting compliments.
• Once rewrote a to-do list so thoroughly it became a tragic novel.

He lives in the mirror realm, where reality is inverted and anxiety is disguised as productivity. Rumour has it he and Gerald share dreams and occasionally swap places just to mess with people.

The Minotaur

A towering figure with a labyrinthine past, the Minotaur is neither fully beast nor man, but a deeply misunderstood guardian of lost truths. Once imprisoned by ancient storytellers in a maze meant to erase his voice, he has since found his way into the Realms not as a monster, but as a symbol of resilience.

The Minotaur speaks rarely, but when he does, his words carry the weight of myth and sorrow. Many forget he is not the original villain in his tale merely a consequence of it. Within his horned head lies ancient knowledge; within his scarred hands, the strength to protect the fragile threads of stories that others would abandon.

Though feared by some, he is revered by those who see through appearances especially by children, animals, and misfit plotlines. He now walks the edges of the Realms, guarding the liminal spaces where memory and meaning blur, and offering refuge to characters too wild for structure.

He wears a rune-branded bracer, a reminder of his past bindings, and a necklace made from broken keys each one a story that once locked him away.

Nyra

Nyra – The Keeper of the Unwritten

Nyra exists between pages, half ink, half possibility. She is a phantom librarian from a realm where stories are born but not yet written. Her robes are made of shifting parchment, and her voice sounds like turning pages in a quiet room. Nyra can sense when a tale is about to vanish from memory and races to save it, trapping it inside glass quills and feathered journals.

Mysterious yet kind, she appears to those who are about to give up on their own story, offering one last plot twist, a final rewrite. Some say she once loved a plotline that betrayed her, and now she trusts only in endings she edits herself. Others whisper that she is the soul of the Author's forgotten drafts.

Nyra doesn't speak in full sentences; she speaks in ellipses, cliffhangers, and poetic fragments. Her eyes glow faintly when a tale is worth saving. When the Realms were nearly destroyed by plot erosion, Nyra arrived unannounced, leaving only one note:

"Stories never truly die... they just wait to be remembered."

Nyric

Nyric is the twin brother of Nyra, born under the pale glow of the Frost Moons. Where Nyra channels stillness and clarity, Nyric pulses with wild energy and ancient memory. He speaks rarely, but when he does, his words are riddles wrapped in prophecy. His eyes carry the weight of too many truths, and his presence has been known to disrupt spells, bend timelines, and awaken long-dormant magic.

Once a celebrated seer of the Fifth Realm, Nyric vanished during the Cracking of the Mirror War. Rumours whispered that he walked into a memory and never returned. That is… until now. He appears again beside his sister, seemingly unchanged, though the very air around him crackles with unstable power.

Nyric's magic is memory-based; he sees the echoes of what was and sometimes what might never be. He is haunted by the idea that he once foresaw the end of the Realms and failed to stop it. Whether that vision was truth or illusion remains unknown.

Odin – Character Bio

Name: Odin
Title: The Allfather (Self-Appointed), CEO of
Wisdom, Coffee, and Overthinking
Also Known As: The Guy on the Tree, Mr. One-
Eyed Dramatic Monologue

Bio:
Odin is the moody, mysterious, monocular
mastermind of the Realms, a god of wisdom, war,
and passive-aggressive prophecy. Known for
trading his eye for knowledge (and bringing it up
at every dinner party), he once spent nine days
hanging from the Tree of Life to learn the secrets
of the runes. What did he gain? Cosmic insight,
yes. But also, joint pain and a lifelong vendetta
against squirrels.

He walks the line between noble leader and
emotionally unavailable drama king. With his
raven informants, cloak of brooding, and beard
that smells faintly of pine and poetry, Odin
believes he sees everything...except his own
blind spots. He loves deeply, but he shows it in a
weird way (like by disappearing for eons). Still,
when the Realms fracture, Odin stands ready to
protect them even if it means rewriting a few
destinies or throwing cryptic riddles at his allies
for no reason.

Special Powers:
- Rune Magic
- Prophecy (unhelpfully vague)
- Animal Telepathy (limited to dramatic birds)
- Guilt-tripping people via ancient poetry

Signature Quote:
"Knowledge is power. But so is knowing when to pretend you didn't hear Loki's latest idea."

Rumour Has It:
He secretly collects teacups with tiny owls on them. Denies it every time.

The tiny owl teacups

Plottie™ – The Plot Child

Title: The Plot Child
Realm of Origin: The Inkwell Between Chapters
Species: Living Idea
Affiliation: The Rewrite Realms
Alignment: Chaotically Creative

Bio:
Plottie™ is not born. She is scribbled into existence the
moment a story begins to wobble off course. Mischievous,
bright-eyed, and slightly smudged with ink, she's the magical
embodiment of narrative mayhem armed with a quill too large
for her and an imagination too big for most story arcs.

She lives in the margins of unwritten pages, chewing on
tropes and giggling through loopholes. Whether she's
shuffling chapters around while you sleep, whispering side
quests into a dragon's ear, or emotionally blackmailing villains
into redemption arcs, Plottie™ thrives in the chaos between
outline and execution.

Despite her size, she's a cosmic force. Powerful enough to
derail an epic saga with one scribble... but often too distracted
by sparkly subplots to finish her own.

Abilities:
- Plot twist conjuration
- Metafictional awareness (she knows she's in a story)
- Unreliable narrator immunity
- Can weaponize foreshadowing
- Immune to writer's block (but causes it in others)

Catchphrase:
"Oopsie! Did I do that... or was that the outline goblin?"

Princess Parenthesis – The Parenthetical Powerhouse

Princess Parenthesis is the elusive punctuation royal who appears (often at the worst possible moment) to clarify, distract, or throw in emotional subtext no one asked for. Wearing a tiara made of commas and a gown stitched from editorial remarks, she has the rare magical ability to interrupt dramatic moments with oddly specific backstory. She's charming, confusing, and always side-tracking the plot.

Her wand? A curved quill that writes only in whispers.
Her nemesis? The dreaded Period (who wants everything to end).
Her dream? To add context to a world that's lost its nuance.

Some say she's the reason no one in the Realms ever gets to the point.
Others say (though this is unconfirmed) she was once an ordinary editor cursed by a grammar goblin.

Princess Rhymelda – Character Bio

Name: Princess Rhymelda
Title: The Bardic Belle of Versetide
Known As: The Rhyme Royal, Keeper of Cadence,
Duchess of Dramatic Pauses

Bio:
Born beneath a crescent moon in the melodic kingdom
of Versetide, Princess Rhymelda speaks almost entirely
in rhyme. Her lullabies can tame dragons, and her
poems have accidentally declared war (twice). With a
golden quill tucked behind one ear and a gown made of
shimmering metaphors, she wanders the Realms,
spreading lyrical confusion and unexpected inspiration.

Though delightful, she's also dangerously dramatic,
once halting a duel with a sonnet so tear-jerking, both
parties hugged it out (then sobbed for three days
straight). She is the sworn poetic rival of Plottie™ and
may or may not be secretly dating a metaphor.

Favourite Quote:
"If I speak in prose, it's cause I'm asleep,
When I'm awake, the rhyming runs deep."

Roarnan – The Quiet Flame

Name: Roarnan, Guardian of the Threshold

Title: The Quiet Flame
Race: Part-Elven, Part-Stormkin
Realm: The Borderlands Between Worlds
First Appearance: Book Two – The Crown and the Thread

Bio

Roarnan is the steadfast and enigmatic guardian who stands watch at the edges of the known realms where stories end, and others dare not begin. He rarely speaks, but when he does, his words weigh heavier than prophecy. Born of lightning and lore, Roarnan once chose exile over allegiance, walking the in-between so others could pass safely into the unknown.

He has a lion's courage, an elf's patience, and a gaze that seems to pierce straight into your future mistakes. While Aurelya suspects he knows more than he lets on, he remains fiercely loyal, so even when the truth aches.

Despite his serious demeanour, he has a soft spot for broken things, lost causes, and any creature that brings snacks.

Notable Abilities

• Can see multiple possible timelines at once, though he hides this well.

• Opens paths that others can't even see.

• Uncannily good at fixing broken compasses, maps, and hearts.

Signature Quote

"Even the strongest flame begins as a spark. But not all sparks are meant to burn.

SIR BROODINGTON III

Sir Broodington III – Character Bio

Sir Broodington III is a deeply serious chicken of noble lineage and considerable emotional weight. He spends most of his time contemplating the existential crisis of being both poultry and poet. Known for his dramatic sighs, long pauses before delivering opinions, and tragic backstory (which he refuses to discuss but alludes to constantly), Sir Broodington is revered among the barnyard literati.

Favourite Quote: "Alas, the yolk is not on them... it is on me."

Hobbies: Moody journaling, long walks in the rain, refusing to be scrambled.

Role in the Realms: The solemn narrator of dramatic recaps and occasional chaos interpreter when Sir Tangent goes too far off track. Fond of Plot Baby, suspicious of Chad's crystals.

Cluckings
of a
Tormented
Soul

Sir Broodington the Third – Character Bio

Name: Sir Broodington the Third
Species: Chicken
Title: The Feathered Philosopher of the Coop

Bio:
Sir Broodington the Third is not to be confused with Sir Broodington III, though he'd be far too melancholic to correct you. A moody poultry with a mind full of metaphors, Sir Broodington the Third spends most of his time gazing wistfully at the rain while composing tragic haikus about corn, betrayal, and the inevitability of the egg.

Wearing a miniature velvet cloak (mostly for the drama), he is the emotional support chicken no one asked for, but everyone somehow ends up confessing their deepest secrets to. He once tried to duel a mirror for "looking too deeply into his soul" and is known to weep softly when someone mentions "free range."

Despite his dramatic nature, his poetry has moved dragons to tears and convinced a troll to pursue interpretive dance. Some say he once sighed so profoundly it caused a small landslide.

Fun Fact:
Carries a tiny notebook titled *"Clucking's of a Tormented Soul."

Sir Tangent the Derailer

Knight of the Long-Winded Order, Slayer of Straightforwardness, and Certified Conversational Cul-de-sac

Once a noble knight with a promising destiny, Sir Tangent took a fateful detour, mid-sentence, and never quite made it back. Known across the Realms for his uncanny ability to derail any discussion, mission, or prophecy with an utterly irrelevant anecdote, he rides a horse named "Anyway" and is followed by a squire whose sole job is to gently nudge him back on topic.

Sir Tangent once interrupted a royal wedding to recount the time he met a talking frog who sold insurance. It had nothing to do with the occasion, but the story took 47 minutes and somehow ended in a musical number.

Despite his distractibility, he is weirdly beloved. His derailments have, accidentally, saved lives, uncovered lost truths, and once prevented a war simply by confusing both sides into calling a truce so they could "circle back later."

He carries a sword, he constantly forgets the name of, and wears armour engraved with footnotes. His personal motto?
"Where was I going with this again?"

Sparkles Roarworthy

Name: Sparkles Roarworthy
Species: Majestic Lion-Dragon Hybrid
Title: The Roar of Radiance

Bio:
Sparkles Roarworthy is the dazzling fusion of two equally
dramatic species, lion and dragon. With a mane that
glistens like morning dew on a disco ball and wings that
shimmer with every colour not yet discovered by human
eyes, Sparkles doesn't just enter a room, he *arrives* with
theme music. He was once mistaken for a comet by a
village of poets and now uses that story to demand only
the finest cushions to sit on.

His roars are said to bring either clarity or spontaneous
interpretive dance—depending on the listener. Loyal to
Aurelya and fiercely protective of snacks, Sparkles can
breathe fire, recite haiku, and nap for 16 hours without
moving a single fabulous whisker.

Known For:
- Summoning magical sparkles mid-battle for dramatic
effect
- Being too fabulous to function during rainstorms
- Having an ongoing rivalry with thunder because it's "too
loud and tacky"

Fun Fact: Sparkles once defeated a villain by
complimenting them so aggressively that they re-evaluated
their life choices and became a baker.

Alignment: Chaotic Flamboyant Good

Sir Whiskerstein the Wise

Madame Nutmancy

Scamper McPlotbite

Baroness Flufftail

The Squirrel Council

Species: Hyper-Intelligent Woodland Rodents
Affiliation: The Realm of Mischief & Nuts
Official Motto: "Order, Acorns, and Overthrow."

Deep within the gnarled branches of the Story Tree, nestled behind a well-concealed door disguised as bark, sits a most curious and powerful governing body the Squirrel Council.

Formed after the Great Walnut Dispute of Chapter Twelve, the Council now oversees the ethical use of plot twists, acorn taxation, and the occasional coup attempt against larger woodland mammals. Led by Chancellor Chestnut, the Council includes:

- Sir Whiskerstein the Wise – Keeper of Forbidden Snack Scrolls
- Madame Nutmancy – Prophetess of Pecans and Plot Holes
- Scamper McPlotbite – Chief Strategist (and suspected double agent)
- Baroness Flufftail Ambassador of Fluffy Diplomacy

The Council maintains tight surveillance over Loki's pet squirrel, Sir Claws-a-Lot, claiming he once smuggled a subplot out of their archives.

Meetings are conducted in rapid squeaks, followed by ceremonial tail swishes and a ritual nut hoarding. Outsiders rarely understand what's going on, but somehow, the Council always ends up in control of something important like the fate of the Realms or the last cookie

SIR SCRIBBLES
PRESIDING JUDGE

Sir Scribbles – Presiding Judge of the Final Rewrite

*Blindfolded. Brilliant. Slightly ink-stained. *

Sir Scribbles is no ordinary octopus. As the impartial, ever-dignified Presiding Judge of the Final Rewrite, this eight-armed arbiter holds the gavel (and six emergency pens) with quiet authority. Bound by a sacred blindfold made of editorial red tape, Sir Scribbles sees nothing and somehow everything.

Renowned for issuing rulings in haiku form and slapping the courtroom floor with dramatic ink when displeased, Sir Scribbles has long served the Realms with fairness, flair, and a suspicious fondness for parentheses. Despite having no visible eyes, Sir Scribbles always seems to know who's lying, rewriting, or hiding a squirrel under their cloak.

When the fate of the narrative hangs by a comma, only one being can untangle the mess:
Sir Scribbles, the Unseen Editor of Truth.

The Sea Witch

Name: The Sea Witch

Title: Keeper of Tides, Whisperer of Drowned Secrets

Realm: The Shattered Shoals, bordering the Forgotten Deep

Appearance:
The Sea Witch cloaks herself in layers of kelp-like silk that drift as though underwater. Her eyes shimmer like storm-lit tidepools, ever-shifting and unknowable. Her voice rolls like waves, calm, coaxing, then crashing.

Personality:
Cryptic and commanding, she speaks in layered riddles and ancient verse. Some say she remembers every word ever whispered by the sea. Others say she forgets on purpose.

Abilities:
• Summons oceanic illusions, tides, and emotional undertows.
• Binds memories into shells, sells them to those who can pay the price.
• Her potion-brewing is unmatched, especially for poisons, love, or truth.

Notable Lore:
Whispers claim the Sea Witch once loved a god of change, chaos, and charm, and maybe still does. But their story sank long ago... and she won't say what truly happened beneath the waves.

Relationship to the Realms:
Neither villain nor ally. She aids those with worthy causes or interesting stories. Many have bargained with her. Few walked away unchanged.

Thor – God of Thunderous Overcompensations

*Hammer-wielding. Goat-trading. Occasionally chicken-befriending. *

Thor, son of Odin, protector of Realms…
and undefeated champion of the "Loudest Entry" awards.

Armed with Mjölnir (which may or may not be on loan from
an emotionally unstable forge),
Thor brings thunder wherever he goes
sometimes on purpose.

A lover of:
- Dramatic weather,
- Battle cries,
- And snacks stolen from banquet tables during other people's
quests.

Recent endeavours include:
- Trading his goats for chickens (don't ask),
- Hosting underground Warhammer tournaments in Valhalla,
- And trying to learn emotional vulnerability (he's at Level 2…
out of 100).

Despite the muscles and mayhem,
Thor is loyal, brave, and a total softie if you catch him near a
cuddlable chicken.

When he's not smashing things,
He's busy pretending he didn't cry during Act Three of the
Rewrite Saga.

EGBERT
THE BRAVE
HAPPY
FEATHORSSDAY

Thor's Chickens – The Feathered Flock of Thunder

*Ten brave birds. One very chaotic henhouse. *

Behold the elite squad of poultry that followed Thor into battle, brunch, and emotional breakdowns. Whether roosting atop Mjölnir or sabotaging Odin's meeting scrolls, these chickens are no ordinary fowl—they are fowl-midable.

The Line-Up: (Photos Left to right).

• Sir Clucks – Knighted for defending the pantry. Sleeps in a helmet.
• Clucks worth – Polite, punctual, and probably smarter than Thor.
• Yolki – Scrambled in the head. Pecks first, asks later.
• Egbert the Brave – Once challenged a Valkyrie to arm-wrestle (he lost, but won respect).
• Mjolnegg – Thinks he is the hammer. Requires constant supervision.
• Cluckabeth – Speaks only in Shakespearean clucks. Dramatic exits are her specialty.
• Snackrifice – Keeps jumping into cooking pots "for glory." No one lets him.
• Feathorsday – Celebrated every Thursday. Even when it's not.
• GlucoChick – Has a suspicious energy level. May have discovered the mead stash.
• Captain Capri – Wears a tiny cape and gives motivational speeches before breakfast.

Together, they are more than just a pecking order. They are The Flock of Thunder.

Feathers will fly. Dramas will unfold. And somewhere, Thor is yelling,
"WHO ATE MY PANCAKES?!"

Trystan – The Reluctant Prince of Plotlines

Once destined to be the romantic hero in a grand tale, Trystan took one look at the narrative arc and promptly walked off the page. He now freelances as a backstory consultant and part-time plot twist delivery service. With tousled hair, a cloak that always billows (even without wind), and a knack for appearing just before a dramatic reveal, Trystan is equal parts charming and emotionally unavailable. Deep down, he's loyal, poetic, and probably hiding an enchanted secret or two, but good luck getting him to admit it.

The Villain Ex

*He ghosted love. Now he haunts the plot. *

He wasn't always evil.
Just misunderstood. And chronically mysterious.
One minute, he's whispering secrets under the stars.
The next, he's rewriting destiny behind your back.

The Villain Ex is the one you swore was "different."
Turns out, he *was* just not in the way you hoped.

Now he's lurking in the background of every
emotionally charged flashback.
He's the reason the Rewrite Realms still need therapy.

Armed with a tragic past, an annoyingly perfect jawline,
and a flair for betrayal,
he claims he's doing it "for the greater good."

Is he redeemable?
Depends on the chapter.
Is he still kind of hot?
Unfortunately, yes.

But one thing's certain:
He left more than a broken heart behind.
He left a villain arc.

Varyn – Character Bio

Name: Varyn
Title: The Starborne Seer
Role in the Realmsverse: Cosmic Guide and Keeper of
Realm Threads

Bio:
Varyn is a celestial being wrapped in the shimmer of
constellations and silence. With eyes that mirror galaxies
and a voice that sounds like distant thunder softened by
stardust, Varyn rarely speaks, but when he does, Realms
listen. He appears when timelines split, destinies blur, or
when a hero needs a reminder that they are not lost, only
becoming.

Neither wholly mortal nor entirely divine, Varyn drifts
between worlds, tugging gently on fate's strings. Many
mistake him for a myth, but those who have met him
describe a presence that feels like standing at the edge of
eternity. He doesn't interfere; he aligns. The stars whisper
to him. And sometimes, he whispers back.

Known For:
- Appearing unannounced during realm quakes
- Reading the stars by touching ancient ruins
- Saying things that don't make sense until it's already too
late or exactly the right time

Secret:
Varyn once rewrote a timeline to save someone he loved,
and the stars have never let him forget it.

Veylion – The Mirror's Shadow

Veylion walks where light fears to follow. Once bound to the truths hidden in reflection, he is now a rogue echo, part oracle, part outlaw. With a cloak stitched from forgotten prophecies and eyes that shimmer like broken glass, Veylion speaks in riddles, truths, and half-lies... and often all three at once.

Some say he was born from the Mirror. Others claim he broke it.

But everyone agrees that when Veylion appears, the story is about to change, whether the characters are ready or not.

Veyrath – The Flame-bound Guardian

Veyrath is Aurelya's dragon, a blazing force of fury, loyalty, and untamed magic. Born from the heart of the last comet to strike the Realms, Veyrath carries the fire of transformation in his breath. Where Veylion sees what is, Veyrath demands what must become.

He does not whisper warnings; he roars truth. Unapologetically bold, he challenges Aurelya when others dare not, pushing her to rise, to choose, and to burn away what no longer serves.

When Veyrath flies, the skies remember. When he lands, the ground listens. And when he speaks... destinies change.

Though often mistaken for a harbinger of destruction, Veyrath is the guardian of necessary endings and even fiercer beginnings.

REALM DWELLERS & GROUPS

Realm Dwellers & Groups

THE
FORGE DWARFS
MAKERS OF MYTH
AND METAL

The Forge Dwarfs – Makers of Myth and Metal

Known as: The Embervein Brotherhood

Head Blacksmith: Grumble Flintthumb

Specialty: Crafting legendary armour, enchanted gear, and structurally questionable goblets

Forged in the belly of the Realm's oldest volcano (which is now a tourist attraction), the Embervein Brotherhood is the finest crew of smiths this side of the Plot Mountains. Known for their exceptional craftsmanship, booming laughter, and refusal to follow safety protocols, these dwarfs can build anything if bribed with enough snacks and a dramatic backstory.

Whether it's Thor's goat armour, Aurelya's ceremonial crown-polisher, or Loki's retractable chaos-suitcase, these dwarfs' workday and night to keep the Realms stylishly armoured and structurally reinforced. Just don't ask about the *Great Flaming Helmet Incident of Book Five*.

Famous Creations:

- The Chicken Combat Harness (now discontinued)

- Flame-etched gauntlets that punch plot holes into existence

- The Armour of Almost-Invisibility (invisible, but very noisy)

Motto:

"If it's not slightly on fire, is it even forged?"

MOUNTAIN
OF
MUFFINS

The Dwarf

Name: Unknown (goes by "The Dwarf" or "Oi, you!")
Title: Head of the Frosted Resistance, Leader of the Bakery
Wars

Backstory:
The Dwarf once ran a peaceful bakery beneath the
Mountain of Muffins—until a rival clan opened a gluten-
free pastry shop next door. What started as a price war
quickly escalated into the infamous Frosting Skirmishes,
leading to the formation of the "Frosted Resistance."
Known for weaponised cupcakes and tactical tarts, The
Dwarf now fights to protect traditional bakery values (and
the secret recipe scrolls).

Traits:
- Height: Compact, but fierce.
- Beard: Braided and dusted with powdered sugar.
- Armour: Apron reinforced with oven mitts.
- Weapon of choice: Dual-wielded rolling pins.

Notable Quotes:
- "That's not a croissant, it's an insult with layers."
- "Prepare to be glazed and confused."

Role in the Realmsverse:
Primarily comic relief with unexpected wisdom. Often
emerges from flour clouds with profound plot insight and a
scone.

Fun Fact:
Once beat Thor in a bake-off. The loser had to wear an
apron labelled "Knead Me."

The Elves – Whisperers of Wonder and Waffles

Elegant, clever, and just a bit dramatic, the Elves of the Ten Realms live beneath glowing trees and sparkling stars. They're famous for crafting magical gadgets, inventing impractical-but-fabulous shoes, and throwing full-moon waffle feasts (with extra glitter syrup, of course).

They speak in rhymes when they're feeling fancy, prank goblins when they're bored, and bake cookies that mysteriously vanish before they cool. No one's ever seen an elf rush; they believe true magic only happens at the exact moment you're about to give up.

- Most likely to:
- Knit a cloak that grants wishes
- Win a staring contest with a squirrel
- Secretly rewrite your shopping list into a riddle

Motto:
"Be graceful. Be curious. And never trust a goblin holding scissors."

Gary

Name: Gary
Title: Realm Transportation Engineer (Unofficial)

Bio:
Gary is not your typical pigeon. Hailing from the Forgotten Realm of Side Quests, Gary once delivered scrolls, potions, and one poorly wrapped cupcake across interdimensional borders. Due to a freak timeline accident (involving a sneeze, a squirrel, and three plot holes), he now serves as the semi-official transportation expert of the Realms.

Though winged, Gary prefers teleporting, dramatic entrances, and making overly loud flapping sounds just to get attention. He wears a monocle that doesn't help him see any better but gives him gravitas when delivering questionable advice.

Rumour has it he was once engaged to a phoenix but ghosted her because he couldn't handle the heat.

Signature Move: Mid-flight existential monologues.

Favourite Snack: Glazed prophecy crumbs.

Status: Feathered, flustered, and fiercely loyal.

Species: Chaos Squirrel (Possibly)

Profile:
Nutters McFluff is an enigma wrapped in fur. Frequently seen with Sir Claws-a-Lot (though it's unclear who's leading who), Nutters is the wildcard companion of Loki and occasional instigator of minor timeline calamities.

Likes:
- Acorns, but only if stolen
- Shiny objects
- Dramatic entrances via windows
- Whispering ominous lore at 3 am

Dislikes:
- Squirrel stereotypes
- Time travel rules
- Any narrative that doesn't include him

Notable Incidents:
- Once rewrote the outcome of a battle by sneezing on the Scroll of Destiny.
- Bit Gerald's evil twin on the ankle for fun. No regrets.

Rumours:
Some say Nutters is actually a fallen cosmic librarian who took squirrel form after an editing dispute with the Author.

Quotes:
"Skreee?" (Often interpreted as either 'I know what you did' or 'I want snacks.')

Alignment: Chaotic Furry-al (furry + feral + possibly ethereal)

BUTTERMUNCH
THE THUNDEROUS

Odin's Goat - Buttermunch the Thunderous

Species: Goat (Allegedly)
Occupation: Odin's Loyal-ish Steed, Snack Enthusiast, and Thunder Consultant

Bio:
Buttermunch the Thunderous is not your average goat. He once licked a lightning bolt out of curiosity and now farts cumulonimbus clouds. With a beard braided by fate (and hay), Buttermunch accompanies Odin into battle, diplomatic events, and buffet lines. Known for headbutting inconsistencies in contracts and chewing on sacred scrolls, he has single-hoofedly derailed nine peace treaties and one family barbecue.

Favourite Activities:
• Headbutting metaphors
• Screaming into the void (for fun)
• Eating important magical documents
• Blaming the other goat for everything

Fun Fact: Buttermunch once swallowed a cursed rune and now occasionally speaks in rhyming riddles when spooked or bored.

Quote: "BAAAAAANG." (The sound he made that one time he tripped into a prophecy.)

The Samurai Otters – Guardians of the Ripple Code

Forged in silence beneath the cherry blossoms of the River Realm, the Samurai Otters are a legendary band of fur-clad warriors who live by the Ripple Code, an ancient philosophy that values honour, mischief, and perfectly timed splashes.

Led by Master Whiskerashi, a one-eyed otter with a bamboo hat and a katana made from the polished rib of a dragonfish, the clan has protected the River Realm from chaos, carp uprisings, and unsolicited poetry slams for centuries. Their code forbids unnecessary violence… but allows for dramatic slow-motion flips and snack-based diplomacy.

Each otter is trained in the Five Sacred Forms:
• Paw of Precision
• Tail of Terror
• Whisker Whispers
• Splash & Dash
• The Legendary Float and Stare

Most feared of all? Their sudden haikus in battle:

"Steel glints in moonlight.
You stole my seaweed again.
Now face the splash, fool."

The Shakespearean Penguins – Troupe of the Frostbitten Bard

Once ordinary performers of the icy south, these dapper, flightless thespians took a wrong turn during a midwinter soliloquy and waddled straight into the Realms. Now, they tour across dimensions as the *Troupe of the Frostbitten Bard*, performing Shakespearean dramas (with dramatic pauses for fish snacks) in impeccable iambic pentameter.

Clad in ruffled collars, velvet capes, and occasionally, fish-scale codpieces, each penguin plays multiple roles depending on the performance: *Macbeth* on Mondays, *Pengu-let* on Thursdays, and the ever-popular *The Tempest (But With More Snow)* on weekends.

Their leader, Sir Beaketh of Bardberg, insists the stage be carved from glacier ice and the audience be sufficiently dramatic. Critics rave: "A triumph of tragic squawking!" – *The Squirrel Times*

Their motto?
"To squawk or not to squawk, that is the flippering question."

SIR
CRUMBS

Sir Crumbs

Sir Crumbs – The Pastry Paladin

Once a humble tart in the Royal Realm of Leftovers, Sir Crumbs rose to knighthood after saving a tea party from total disaster. With a flaky crust, a gooey centre of heroism, and a blade forged from a dessert fork, Sir Crumbs defends justice one crumb at a time.

He is valiant in the face of kitchen chaos and has a sworn oath to never go stale while duty calls. He's also slightly emotionally scarred from being mistaken for a scone at the Great Bake-Off Battle of Realm 3.

Allies say Sir Crumbs smells faintly of vanilla courage and powdered sugar valour. His greatest weakness? Hot coffee and being left unattended near the squirrel.

Spikeston the Impenetrable

Name: Spikeston the Impenetrable

Title: Sentinel of the Snack Vault

Species: Armoured Porcupine (with a heart of gold and quills of justice)

Role:
Spikeston is the steadfast and slightly overdramatic guard of the Squirrel Council's most treasured secret, the Snack Vault. Tasked with ensuring not a single nut, raisin, or cheddar biscuit escapes unauthorised nibbling, he has trained in the ancient martial arts of Pointy Poke-Fu and Snack-Fu Defence Tactics.

Known For:
• Refusing to blink until every threat is neutralised (his record is 6.5 hours).
• Once tackled a suspicious leaf.
• Declared a walnut "suspiciously smug" and placed it in solitary confinement.

Appearance:
Donning a spiked armour that is mostly his own back, Spikeston's presence is both prickly and noble. His deep-set eyes scan every movement, and his dramatic pauses during council meetings are legendary.

Weakness:
Struggles with stairs and has a soft spot for tragic opera.

Quote:
"If you touch the Cheddar Hoard, you answer to me… and my quills."

The Giants – Gentle Hulks of the High Hills

Realm: The Cloud Top Crags

The Giants are enormous, kind-hearted, and famously terrible at whispering. They live in the highest mountains where clouds tickle their toes and goats teach them yoga (don't ask). Despite their size, they're surprisingly gentle unless someone steals the last cookie.

Each Giant has a special talent: one knits scarves as long as rivers, another sings lullabies that make volcanoes nap, and one invented a trampoline big enough for a moon bounce.

- Most likely to:
- Mistake a dragon egg for a pebble
- Host a tea party with thunderclaps
- Sleep through an avalanche (again)

Motto:
"Speak loud, hug big, and always double-check before sitting down."

The Masked Ones

*They speak in echoes. They move like memory. *

No one knows where they came from.
Not even them.

The Masked Ones drift at the edges of the Realms, shadows
shaped like people, wearing masks made of other people's
expectations. Some masks smile. Some frown. Some crack
under the weight of pretending.

They don't talk.
They reflect.

If you stare too long, you might see yourself.
Not as you are but as you were when you stopped being
honest.

The Masked Ones don't mean harm.
They only mirror what's hidden.
Regret. Fear. Dreams left behind.

Some say they guard the places between stories.
Others say they were once characters… rewritten until
they forgot who they were.

But if you listen closely, when one passes by,
you might hear a whisper:

"Take off the mask.
Or you'll forget your face too."

REALLY?
THAT'S YOUR
PLAN?

The Talking Cactus

*Prickly advice. Surprisingly profound. *

No one planted it.
No one remembers when it arrived.
And yet, there it stands right in the middle of pivotal scenes,
offering unsolicited opinions with a sarcastic drawl.

The Talking Cactus has been called many things:
• The Thorn of Truth
• The Oracle of Ouch
• That Annoying Plant That Won't Stop Narrating

But don't be fooled by the sass.
Its barbs often cut to the heart of things metaphorically *and* literally.

Some say it was once a great philosopher cursed by a plot twist.
Others think it's just a cactus with an attitude and excellent timing.

Whatever the case, if you're on a quest, expect it to chime in:
"Really? That's your plan?"

Because the Talking Cactus may be rooted,
but it always finds a way to stir things up.

THE WITNESSES

The Witnesses

*They do not interfere. They remember. *

Scattered across the Realms like forgotten echoes,
The Witnesses are always present but never seen in full.
Not by choice.
By design.

They are the silent record-keepers.
Eyes that blink between timelines.
Voices that never speak, only hum with memory.

Each one appears differently:
a raven perched on a windowsill,
a child drawing spirals in the dirt,
a flicker in the corner of a mirror.

They are not gods.
They are not mortals.
They are something older.
Bound to observe every rewrite,
and carry the cost of knowing what *could have been.*

If you ever feel like you're being watched by a moment
itself...
you are.

The Witnesses were there.
They always are.

The Time-Tossed Jury

*Justice... eventually. *

They were summoned for one day.
They've been deliberating for centuries.

Composed of twelve utterly incompatible members, the
Time-Tossed Jury includes:
- A Victorian ghost who insists on speaking in riddles,
- A sentient hourglass with commitment issues,
- An unpaid intern from the future,
- A squirrel in a robe (identity disputed),
- And seven other jurors whose timelines contradict
each other, often mid-sentence.

Bound to deliver a verdict on "What Even Happened?",
They've reviewed every rewrite, flashback, paradox, and
plot twist.

Consensus? Elusive.
Snacks? Limited.
Existential dread? High.

They may never agree
But when they finally do...
the ruling echoes across Realms.

The Time-Tossed Jury:
Out of sync, but never out of order.

Mascot Bio – Closure the Cloaked Raccoon

Mascot: Closure the Cloaked Raccoon
Title: Emotional Support Mascot (Unofficial but deeply respected)

Closure is the unofficial mascot of The School for Emotionally Unavailable Side Characters a wise, cloaked raccoon who's seen more character arcs than most protagonists. He carries a satchel filled with tissues, half-finished poetry, and a well-worn copy of "Attachment Styles for Sidekicks." Despite his beady eyes and suspicious snack hoarding, Closure offers sage advice at the most inconvenient (but narratively perfect) moments.

Students often whisper that he's lived through at least twelve tragic love stories, two redemption arcs, and one overly dramatic enemies-to-lovers subplot. He never confirms. He just adjusts his cloak and disappears into the drama.

Slogan

"Be dramatic. Just not self-destructive."
The school motto, embroidered on every cloak, tea mug, and trauma support pillow in the dormitory lounge.

Spiny the Bartender – Keeper of Drinks and Secrets

Spiny is not your average barkeep. A small, round hedgehog-like creature with impeccable posture and sharper wit than his spines, Spiny runs the tavern with a blend of sarcasm and sincerity that keeps even the gods in check.

He serves brews that fizz with truth serum and cocktails that rewrite memories, though he never drinks his own concoctions. With a perfectly groomed moustache (yes, somehow) and a ledger full of unpaid emotional tabs, Spiny is known for pouring just the right drink at the wrong moment... or was it the other way around?

He's also Loki's unofficial therapist, official accountant, and occasional babysitter of the squirrel. Just don't ask what's really in the "Heartbreak on the Rocks" special.

Signature Quote:
"Life's messy. That's why I serve it stirred, not shaken."

Whiffles

Title: The Whispering Puff of Mischief

Species: Unknown (possibly cloud? Possibly sentient sneeze?)

Realm: Frequently found where seriousness is at risk of being too serious.

Whiffles is a floating puffball of unpredictable joy, equal parts fluff, glitter, and chaos. Nobody knows where Whiffles came from. One moment, the Realms were full of solemn prophecy and world-ending stakes, and the next... Whiffles. He smells faintly of marshmallows, occasionally sparks confetti when startled, and drifts wherever laughter is needed most.

Although dismissed by some as a "plot-distraction," Whiffles has been known to unlock secret passages, expose villain monologues, and once saved the day by sneezing on a time curse.

Is he a pet? A spirit? A snack that gained sentience? No one knows. But if Whiffles nuzzles up to you and emits a soft "whuff," your day is about to get interesting.

REALM
LOCATIONS

Real Locations

THE TREE OF LIFE

The Tree of Life

*Rooted in every realm. Reaching toward every rewrite.
*

It stands at the centre of all things seen and unseen.

Its roots curl through timelines.
Its branches brush against dreams.
Its leaves whisper forgotten truths to those brave
enough to listen.

The Tree of Life is not just alive.
It *remembers.*

It remembers the first word ever written.
The first story ever told.
The first realm that bloomed and the first one that fell.

Legends say each leaf holds a story.
Each branch, a path not taken.
Each falling petal, a warning.

Some seek its wisdom.
Others seek to control it.
But no one not even the Author writes without its
shadow watching.

Because the Tree doesn't just grow stories.
It guards them.

THE BOOK TREE

The Book Tree

*Where stories sleep and secrets root deep. *

High on a hill no map remembers stands The Book Tree, a living library grown from forgotten dreams and half-finished tales. Its bark is etched with inked verses. Its leaves flutter with unwritten pages. Its roots whisper in rhymes.

When the wind blows just right, you can hear it hum lullabies written by authors who never got to say the end.

No one knows who planted the first story. But it is said that every time someone lets go of a tale too heavy to carry, the Book Tree catches it. Tucks it in a branch. And waits.

Some books are wild and keep growing sideways. Some are stubborn and fall off five times before they stay. Some are so full of emotion, they bloom into blossom-chapters overnight.

The Book Tree doesn't judge. It simply holds space. For every ending, still becoming.

The Library

A seemingly infinite space stacked with stories, truths, lies, and everything in between. The library isn't just a place, it's a living entity with a personality as old as time and twice as moody. It grows new wings with every unwritten ending and occasionally eats chapters that displease it. Books whisper secrets, staircases shift when no one's looking, and somewhere, buried beneath the dust of forgotten stories, is the answer to a question no one dares to ask.

THE SCHOOL FOR
EMOTIONALLY-
UNAVAILABLE SIDE
CHARACTERS

The School for Emotionally Unavailable Side Characters

The School for Emotionally Unavailable Side Characters Location: Somewhere between a plot twist and a repressed memory.

Tucked between forgotten footnotes and unspoken confessions lies an exclusive institution designed for those who never got their emotional arcs or deliberately dodged them. This elite boarding school accepts only the most commitment-phobic, emotionally distant, sarcastically defensive, or tragically avoidant supporting characters.

Run by a former plot device who once dated a main character and never got closure, the school specialises in:
- Advanced Deflection
- Deep Sighing 101
- "I'm Fine" Masterclasses
- Doorway Brooding
- Electives in Accidental Vulnerability (attendance optional)

Despite their collective reluctance, students often graduate with unfinished business, a single tear they pretend was allergies, and a diploma they insist they "don't need."

Rumour has it even a few fan-favourite villains audit the evening classes.

"The Misrule Inn" – Loki's Tavern

Type: Interdimensional Gathering Place

Proprietor: Loki (obviously)

Specialties:

- Chaotic cocktails

- Ever-changing décor

- Nonsense riddles that somehow make sense after 3 drinks

- A guestbook that bites

- Live performances by sentient furniture (Tuesdays only)

Description:

Loki's Tavern exists outside of linear time and space but somehow always near the worst decisions. The Misrule Inn welcomes rogues, romantics, and plot holes with equal enthusiasm. Here, spilled drinks rewrite destinies, bar brawls solve existential riddles, and every guest leaves with a different version of what happened. No one remembers arriving, but no one ever wants to leave.

The décor shifts based on the emotional mood of the patrons. One moment it's velvet-cloaked and candlelit, the next it's a neon nightmare with disco trolls. The rules are simple:
- Lie creatively
- Tip generously
- Don't ask about the raccoon in charge of inventory

Rumour Has It:

A portal to the 4th plot wall opens behind the keg when the house band plays Loki's Lament backward.

EMOTIONAL
BAGGAGE

A Ship Named Emotional Baggage – Vessel of Chaotic Healing

Name:

A Ship Named Emotional Baggage

Type:

Sentient Sea Vessel / Floating Therapy Session / Pirate-Adoption-Cruiser

Captain:

Varies. Frequently commandeered by Chad or Belladonna, sometimes by no one at all.

Known For:

• Haunted by echoes of past trauma (and occasionally, karaoke).
• Below deck contains a labyrinth of locked trunks, each labelled with unresolved plot arcs.
• Rumoured to weep quietly at sunset.
• Has very firm opinions on everyone's coping mechanisms.

Alliances & Conflicts:

• Sworn to the Realms, but only if they're willing to talk about their feelings.
• Once crashed into a cliff to make a point.
• Passive-aggressive toward other ships with cooler names.

Notable Quote (from the ship's bell):

"Ding ding. You're avoiding your emotional growth again."

Realmsverse Note:

While its origins are unclear, this ship is now an official vessel of the Rewrite Realms. Those who board rarely leave unchanged (or fully dry-eyed). Despite its sass, it's strangely reliable — as long as you're willing to unpack your baggage... one trunk at a time.

Magical Items & Events

Magical Items & Events

The Scroll

*It doesn't just record history. It dares to rewrite it. *

The Scroll is not paper.
It is time, folded.
It is truth, inked in metaphors.

Whispered to have been spun from threads of fate and
bound in dragon light,
The Scroll records the Realms not as they are, but as
they choose to become.

Every tale ever told is written there.
Every ending still possible waits in the margins.

Some say it is infinite.
Others say it simply rewrites itself when no one's
looking.

The Scroll is guarded by no lock,
but only those who belong to the story may open it.

Unrolling it reveals more than plot twists.
It reveals the reader.

Because The Scroll doesn't show you the truth.
It shows you what you're afraid to believe.

The Mirror

*It shows what the story tried to hide. *

The Mirror doesn't lie.
It doesn't flatter.
It doesn't speak.

It simply reflects what's already there
The fears scribbled between the lines.
The strength disguised as softness.
The endings someone tried to erase.

No one knows who made The Mirror,
only that it appears when a character is ready to face a
truth too sharp to name.

It has no agenda.
No opinion.
Just clarity.

Some who look into The Mirror see monsters.
Others see memories.
A few see themselves for the first time.

But all who look...
must choose what to do with what they see.

Because The Mirror doesn't change the story.
It just shows you how it was always meant to be.

The Author's Mirror

*The reflection that remembers what she
forgets.*

Tucked inside the quiet corners of the page lives
The Author's Mirror, a soft-spoken reflection who
holds the pieces The Author leaves behind.

She doesn't speak in paragraphs.
She whispers in pauses.
In scribbled-out thoughts and unsent letters.
In the shimmer of ink that never quite dried.

When the Author grows tired, the Mirror listens.
When The Author doubts, the Mirror steadies.
And when the story begins to fade
The Mirror remembers the words she meant to
say.

Though made of glass and memory, The Author's
Mirror is no illusion.
She is gentle truth.
Quiet power.
And the keeper of the words behind the words.

The Thread

*One line. Infinite consequences. *

It is not woven.
It weaves.

The Thread runs through every tale, every
choice, every whispered "what if."
Sometimes gold. Sometimes shadow.
Always pulling.

To some, it appears as fate.
To others, a curse.
But to the Realms themselves it is memory
stitched into time.

Those who touch the Thread may glimpse…
A past they forgot.
A future not yet written.
A version of themselves that could have been.

But beware:
Tug too hard, and the whole story unravels.

Because The Thread doesn't break.
It rewrites.

The Prophecy Eggs

*Cracked open once. Never the same again. *

No one remembers who laid them.
Not even the creatures who guard them.

The Prophecy Eggs shimmer with ink-light, their
shells etched in ancient runes no one dares
translate out loud. Each egg holds a prophecy but
only the one who cracks it will know if that
future is a blessing, a burden… or a very
confusing metaphor.

They hum with unwritten stories.
They rattle when a lie is told nearby.
And if one begins to glow?
You'd best start rewriting your schedule and
your fate.

Some say the Eggs choose their moment.
Others say they hatch when reality hiccups.

But one truth remains:

Once a Prophecy Egg opens,
nothing goes back in

The Tapas Table

*Feeding plot points since Volume 2. *

It began as a humble snack station.

Now?
It's a sentient buffet with opinions, a seating plan, and diplomatic immunity.

The Tapas Table appears in moments of chaos, conflict, or contemplation, offering perfectly portioned bites that always seem *weirdly relevant* to the moment.

Mushroom tart for bravery.
Olive skewers for secrets.
A suspiciously glowing dip for existential dread.

Some believe the Table is older than the Realms themselves.
Others think it's just a catering hallucination brought on by too many rewrites.

But one thing is certain:
Wherever destiny gathers... so do the snacks.

Because no great plot twist ever happened on an empty stomach.

A Mood Ring

Classification: Enchanted Elf Accessory

(Possibly cursed. Definitely, Dramatic.)

Originally crafted by an overly emotional elf during a poetry recital gone wrong, the Mood Ring is no ordinary jewellery. It doesn't just react to your feelings, it reacts to everyone's feelings within a five-muffin radius.

It glows purple near mystery, turns orange when snacks are imminent, and turns black when someone's trying to lie about not eating the last cookie. Occasionally, it spins wildly when someone has a secret crush. Or gas.

Nobody really knows what the colours mean. Even the ring isn't sure. It just wants to be included.

- Most likely to:
- Panic during a group hug
- Spark an accidental proposal
- Ruin a surprise party by glowing neon green in advance

Warning:
May emotionally bond with your finger forever.

The Glitter Bomb

Classification: Fairy-Class Item (also banned from Goblin Parliament)

Created by accident during a fairy dance-off, the Glitter Bomb is now a popular, if slightly unpredictable, way to express extreme emotion, mark a celebration, or dramatically exit a conversation.

A single clap, a spark of mischief, and BOOM!
Confetti. Everywhere.
Sparkles in your hair for seven years.
And someone's shoes are now rainbow-colored.
(Even if they weren't wearing shoes.)

It's rumoured that one Squirrel Council member once set off three glitter bombs in a row. We still can't find the sky.

- Most likely to:
- Turn a battle into a birthday party
- Be hidden inside someone's teacup
- Cause a unicorn to sneeze rainbows

Warning:
Not suitable for use near sandwiches, sleeping dragons, or anyone who says, "Keep it down."

The Enchanted Crayons

"Not all magic requires ink. Just attitude."

Born from the aftermath of the Great Crayon Rebellion, these vibrant little artifacts are scattered across the Realms. Each Enchanted Crayon holds a unique and occasionally unstable magical ability; they're used, feared, and frequently confiscated by the Squirrel Council.

No two sets are the same, and their enchantments are unpredictable:
- Red draws literal fire.
- Blue temporarily erases gravity.
- Purple translates everything into dramatic poetry.
- Yellow's effect is unknown. No one has survived long enough to explain it.

Capable of redrawing fate lines, reshaping ceilings, and doodling on destiny, they are banned in most libraries and classified by the Rewrite Court as 'narratively unstable.'

- Most likely to:
- Unleash chaos during nap time
- Vandalise a prophecy mid-scroll
- Summon a dragon wearing a tutu (by accident)

Warning:
May cause spontaneous art attacks, timeline distortion, and emotional doodling.

CHAD'S THERAPY CRYSTALS™

truthstone

Forces radical honesty.
Often misused.

blush quartz

Makes people feel like
they've just been hugged.
Sometimes weeps

ambiguite

For "when you're not
ready to heal,
but you're vibing."

plotite

Flashes when someone
is being overly dramatic

Chad's Therapy Crystals™

Type:

Magical Object / Questionably Calibrated Mental Health Aid

Origin:

"Found them under a ley line. Or a couch." – Chad

Known For:

Glowing at inconvenient emotional moments. Humming when someone is lying to themselves. Once started vibrating during Gerald's confession and exploded into glitter.

Crystal Types & Their "Certified" Uses:

Truth stone – Forces radical honesty. Often misused.
Blush Quartz – Makes people feel like they've just been hugged. Sometimes weeps.
Ambiguite – For 'when you're not ready to heal, but you're vibing.'
Plotite – Flashes when someone is being overly dramatic. Yes, it glows near Loki a lot.

Realmsverse Note:

Chad insists the crystals are "attuned to the emotional resonance of your unresolved inner subplots." No one knows what that means. But they *do* seem to work.

Legendary Weapons & Artefacts

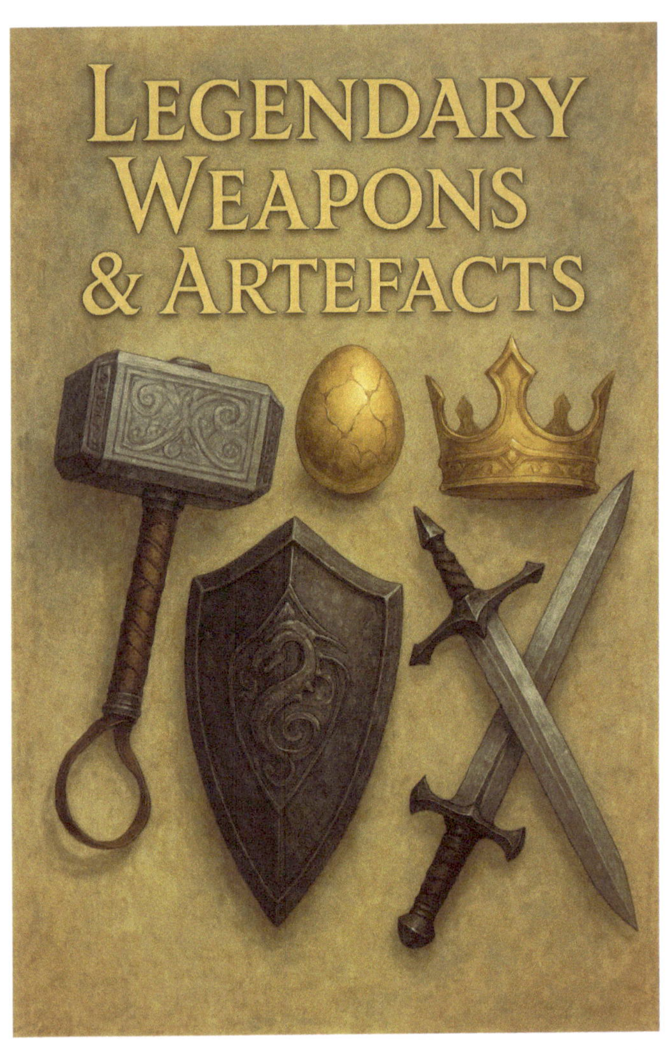

Legendary Weapons & Artefacts

The Pen

*It doesn't write. It remembers. *

The Pen is older than ink.
Older than words.
Older than the first story ever told around a fire.

No one owns The Pen.
It appears when a rewrite must be written, when the
tale has twisted too far from truth.

It doesn't just craft endings.
It holds them back until they're ready.

In the wrong hands, it has started wars between realms.
In the right ones, it has healed wounds no sword could
touch.

The Pen cannot lie.
But it can be silenced.

And when it is...
Stories stall.
Characters forget.
And the Realms begin to unravel.

To hold The Pen is to carry the weight of a thousand
possible truths.
To write with it is to choose just one.

The Pen of Obsidian

Title: The Pen of Obsidian
Also Known As: The Void Quill, The Rewriter's Edge,
Doom-Ink

Role in the Realmsverse:
An ancient artifact crafted from molten obsidian and inked
with stardust and forgotten truths. The Pen of Obsidian
holds the power to rewrite reality, erase history, or forge
new destinies, but at an unspeakable price.

It is not merely a tool, but a sentient artifact, whispering
temptations to those who wield it. The Pen does not serve
the writer it tests them, bending to their will only if they
prove worthy... or broken enough to lose everything.

Powers & Traits:
- Can rewrite events across any of the Ten Realms
- Glows faintly when a truth is about to be undone
- Drips ink only when a soul is at stake
- May only be used once before demanding a memory in
return

Known Users:
- The Narrator (allegedly used to alter the Ending once)
- Aurelya (briefly, during the Rewrite War)
- Unknown others who were never seen again

Warnings:
"This is not a pen. This is a blade disguised as beauty."
 Inscribed on its obsidian case in vanished runes

The Sentient Sword

*It doesn't serve. It chooses. *

Forged from a fallen star and quenched in the ink of
forgotten tales,
The Sentient Sword is more than a weapon, it is a
character.

It hums when destiny draws near.
It glows when truth is spoken.
And it bites harder when someone lies.

The Sword has been wielded by heroes, villains, and
one deeply confused squirrel.
But never for long.
Because it cannot be held, only borrowed.

It whispers to those who carry it.
Not words, but feelings.
A pull. A pressure. A path.

And when it is lost?

The Realms tremble.

Because the Sentient Sword is not looking for power.
It's looking for someone worthy of the final rewrite.

Mjölnir

Name: Mjölnir
Also Known As: The Thunderer's Pride, The Bonk of Justice, That Thing Thor Won't Stop Talking About

Overview:
Mjölnir isn't just a hammer, it's *the* hammer. Forged by dwarves, enchanted by cosmic forces, and wielded by Thor with both flair and frequent overkill, Mjölnir is the Realms' most famous implement of smiting.

Appearance:
Short-handled due to a slight crafting mishap, but still wildly intimidating. Covered in ancient Norse runes that glow when righteous fury (or mild irritation) is present.

Abilities:
- Returns to Thor's hand no matter where it's thrown, even if tossed in a tantrum.
- Only those deemed worthy can lift it (which includes a surprisingly low bar in Realm Ten).
- Capable of summoning lightning, thunder, and dramatic wind for entrances.

Backstory:
Forged by Brokkr and Eitri, Mjölnir was meant to be the perfect weapon. Thanks to Loki's shenanigans, it ended up a little short, but still deadly. It's had many adventures, a few identity crises, and once got stuck in a tree for three weeks.

Fun Fact:
It once rejected Thor during an emotional meltdown, instead choosing to hang out with the family goat for emotional support.

Current Status:
Happily reunited with Thor, although it's recently shown signs of sass. Occasionally glows when lies are told in its presence, especially by Loki.

Rumours:
- Has its own secret side-quest storyline.
- May be dating the sentient broom from Realm Seven

The Crown

*It never fit quite right. *

Once forged to rule, now worn to remember, The Crown is
more than metal and myth. It is memory. It is weight. It is
the quiet ache of every choice made to protect what
matters.

The Crown does not sparkle.
It burns.
With every hope.
Every loss.
Every word left unsaid.

Those who wear it are not chosen by blood, but by burden.
And the moment it rests upon their head, something
changes.
They speak a little less.
They carry a little more.

Some say The Crown listens.
Others say it judges.
But the truth is simpler:
The Crown keeps records.

Of sacrifices.
Of stories.
Of souls.

It doesn't demand loyalty.
It just remembers who gave it anyway.

BONUS
LORE
&
SECRET
LORE

Bonus Lore & Secret Lore

Deleted Characters
Unwritten, Unhinged, and Unapologetically Cut

Lady Metaphoria

"She was a metaphor for metaphors. It got confusing."

• Wore a hat that changed meaning based on context.
• Deleted after she gave a five-page speech that no one understood, including the author.

Sir Tangent the Derailer

• A knight who could not stay on topic.

• Originally meant to narrate side quests.

• Caused three timeline collapses by asking "but what if?" during a prophecy.

The Typo Beast

- Accidentally summoned when Gerald misspelled 'dragon.'
- Had six "noses" and zero grammar.
- Corrected only after devouring an entire page of exposition.

Gerald's Evil Twin, Jerald

- Wore the same hat, but upside down.
- Rejected for being 'too emotionally available.'
- Still appears in the margins of certain editions.

Aunt Clarabelle

- Gave good advice.
- Entirely incompatible with the Realmsverse tone.
- Was written out for being 'too functional.'

Deleted Selves

Deleted Selves
Alias: Echoes of What Was

Bio:
The Deleted Selves are spectral fragments of characters who were rewritten, forgotten, or erased from existence, left behind in the margins of the Realms. They flicker like broken memories, glitching between timelines, whispering "remember me" to no one in particular. Some were plotlines discarded mid-chapter. Others were once main characters, overwritten by new arcs and shinier roles.

Though fragmented and fading, they still carry remnants of their purpose. A catchphrase. A look. A haunting need to finish their story.

Habitat:
They haunt abandoned libraries, half-rendered dreamscapes, and deleted scenes. Some have found refuge in The Library That Eats Endings. Others rally in shadowed corners of The Rewrite Realms, waiting for a second chance or closure.

Notable Quirk:
Speak only in unfinished sentences or dialogue last spoken before deletion.
Examples:
- "But I was going to"
- "You promised we'd"
- "Please, don't forget to…"

Symbol: A fading ink quill mid-stroke.

NO MORE LINES
DOWN WITH BLUE

The Crayons Rebel

Classification: Historical Event (Now taught in Goblin Art Class Level 2)

Once upon a scribble, the crayons had had enough.
They were tired of colouring in the lines, tired of drawing only trees, and especially tired of being chewed on by baby trolls.

Led by Sir Scribble of Cerulean, the crayons snuck out of their box at midnight and launched a full-scale artistic uprising. They covered the moon in polka dots, gave unicorns new hairstyles, and turned the King's official scroll into a comic strip.

Some say the rebellion was chaotic. Others say it was a masterpiece. Either way, no one has been able to find the brown crayon since.

- Most likely to:
- Draw a moustache on the Queen
- Decorate a dragon
- Replace battle maps with doodles of snacks

Warning:
Will scribble on your destiny if left unattended.

This one is...
a READER

This one is... a Reader

*They crossed no portals. Yet they hold every realm. *

Unlike the heroes who clash with gods,
Or the villains who rewrite fate
The Reader never lifted a sword.
But they've carried every character.

They cried in Chapter Three.
Laughed in Chapter Seven.
Paused in Chapter Ten just to whisper, "No. Don't do
it."

They are the only ones who know
how it all felt.

The Realms were never meant to reach them.
And yet... somehow, they always do.

Each page turned echoes louder than any prophecy.
Every highlight, every tear-stain, every re-read
is a kind of magic that not even the Author can
explain.

This one is... a Reader.
The quietest character.
And the most powerful of all.

The Author – Just a Woman

Volume 3: War Beneath the Story

She doesn't wear armour.
She doesn't carry a sword.
She wields a pen.

In a realm where legends clash and gods rewrite fate,
The Author remains something simpler, yet far more
dangerous. She's just a woman who remembers
everything. The forgotten truths. The quiet betrayals.
The stories that were buried beneath louder voices.

She does not shout to be heard.
She writes.

Every word she inks is a rebellion. Every silence she
breaks is a spell. She bleeds across the page with
grace, fury, and precision, reweaving destinies others
tried to unravel.

And though others may try to claim the narrative,
twist it, or erase her entirely...
She always returns.
One chapter stronger.

Because she is not just a woman.
She is The Author.
And the story isn't over.

The Forgotten Gerald

*He was never supposed to be the main character. *

Gerald wasn't written in.
He just... showed up.
Somewhere between Chapter Three and the coffee stain on Page Nine.

He doesn't have a backstory.
Or a destiny.
Or even a proper wardrobe (unless you count the bathrobe made of footnotes).

And yet he's still here.

The Forgotten Gerald lives between the margins.
He rescues lost plot points, feeds misplaced metaphors, and sometimes talks to punctuation like they're old friends.

No one remembers why he was forgotten.
Not even Gerald.
But that hasn't stopped him from helping other stories find their ending.

Because sometimes the characters you forget...
are the ones who never forget you.

The Narrator

*Not seen. Not named. But always there. *

The Narrator is not a character
And yet, they know every character's secrets.
They never walk on stage.
But they hold the spotlight.

Some say the Narrator is a whisper from the First Rewrite.
Others believe it's The Author in disguise.
But the truth?

The Narrator watches.
From between the sentences.
From just behind the fourth wall.
And every now and then...
They lean a little too close.

They've laughed at tragic moments.
Paused for dramatic effect.
And once argued with a footnote for three entire pages.

The Narrator doesn't follow the rules.
They bend them.
Twist them.
Sometimes, break them just for fun.

But one thing is always true:

If the story is still being told...
The Narrator is still watching.

Final Pages – Realmsverse Codex

Acknowledgments

To everyone who believed in wild ideas, stayed up too late with story theories, or just nodded politely while I explained how a raccoon in a cloak is definitely canon, thank you. Special thanks to the Realms themselves, who wrote most of this and only mildly threatened me into finishing it.

About the Author

Holly Symons is the overly caffeinated scribe of the Realmsverse who still insists it all actually happened. She can often be found muttering plotlines to herself, hoarding magical stationery, and correcting reality's continuity errors. When not writing, she's definitely not making deals with goblins for story ideas. Probably.

Further Reading or What's Next

Coming soon: Realmsverse Tales for Troublemakers, a collection of bedtime stories for readers who don't want to sleep. Also look out for 'The Rewrite Realms' novel series and 'Tales from the Ten Realms' for younger adventurers.

Join the Realmsverse fandom at: www.realmsverse.com or follow

@RealmsverseOfficial on socials. We're mostly chaos, occasionally coherent.

Reader Invitation or Thank You

You've survived the Codex. We hope you're only slightly traumatised. If your brain is full of plot holes, emotional damage, and unresolved squirrel-related questions, you're one of us now.

Come back soon. The Realms are always rewriting.

Bonus: Realmsverse Fan Checklist

- Witnessed the Glitter Bomb Incident

- Wondered if Clarence is just a cat

- Suspect Chad forged his goblin credentials

- Tried to summon a tap-dancing squirrel council

- Believed in The Thread, then immediately doubted it

- Argued with a magical item (and lost)

- Questioned your own continuity

www.ingramcontent.com/pod-product-compliance
Lightning Source LLC
Chambersburg PA
CBHW042034180726
48295CB00006B/98